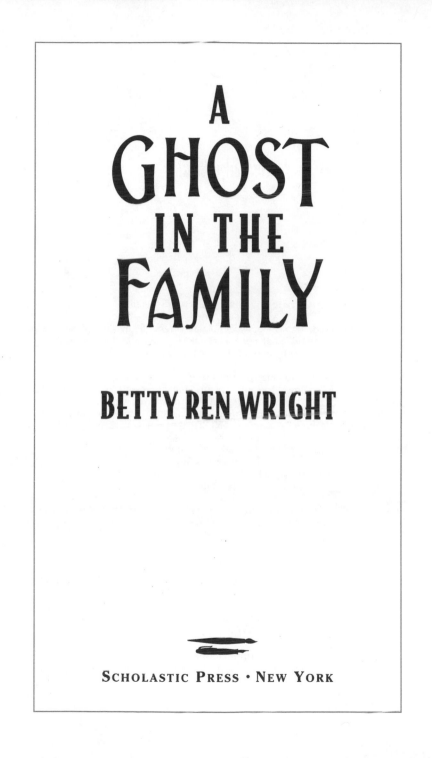

# A
# GHOST
## IN THE
# FAMILY

## BETTY REN WRIGHT

SCHOLASTIC PRESS • NEW YORK

# For Karlee Gauchel

Library of Congress Cataloging-in-Publication Data
Wright, Betty Ren
A Ghost in the Family / Betty Ren Wright
p. cm.

Summary: While visiting his friend Jeannie's eccentric Aunt Rosebud in a boarding house that may be haunted, ten-year-old Chad comes across a mystery involving a missing diamond bracelet.

ISBN 0-590-02955-X
[1. Ghosts — Fiction.   2. Haunted Houses — Fiction   3. Aunts — Fiction.   4. Boardinghouses — Fiction   5. Mystery and detective stories.]   I. Title
PZ7.W933Gefh [Fic] — Dc21  1998  97-22157  CIP  AC

1 3 5 7 9 10 8 6 4 2
8 9/9 0/0 01 02 03

Printed in the U.S.A
First edition, March 1998

# Contents

# ONE

## "You'd Better Not Laugh!"

He was trapped.

Chad Weldon leaned back in the leather seat and scowled as the bus rumbled onto Main Street. Gormans' Furniture Store drifted past the window, then the Spot-Not Laundromat, the Four Star Video Store, and the Dairy Queen. Bristol looked different from the high window of the bus, as if it were no longer Chad's own town. His chest ached at the thought.

At the end of Main Street the bus clattered over the planks of the Green River bridge and picked up speed. They were passing Riverside Park. Chad pressed his forehead against the window, hoping to catch a glimpse of his dad, who worked for the Bristol Park Maintenance Board — mostly cutting grass, trimming trees, and painting picnic tables. But the park slid by swiftly, and then the bus roared up the ramp to the highway. All of Bristol was left behind, except, of course, for Jeannie Nichols. She sat in the seat next to him, whistling through her teeth and working a word search puzzle. She was the one who had gotten him into this mess.

It had been a perfectly good summer vacation until a few days ago. Then Aunt Elsa had announced that she wanted to go to Duluth to visit an old friend who was sick. Chad was shocked. Aunt Elsa belonged with him and his dad. She had come to live with them when his mother died four years ago, and since then, she'd never been away for more than a day.

At breakfast the next morning, Chad had waited uneasily for her to mention going away again. When she didn't, he decided she'd forgotten about it. That was when Jeannie had appeared at the back door, looking ready to pop with excitement.

"I'm going to Milwaukee to visit my Aunt Rosebud for two weeks," she announced. "And she says I can bring a friend with me. So I'm inviting *you,* Chad Weldon!"

"I'm busy," Chad said like a shot. But then he saw Aunt Elsa and his dad look at each other across the table, and his heart sank. They already knew about this invitation. Jeannie's mother must have called them first.

"Well, aren't you the lucky boy!" his dad exclaimed. "Fun in the big city!"

"That's very nice of you, Jeannie dear," Aunt Elsa said. "I'm going to be away for a while, and we've been wondering who would look after Chad during the day."

No one seemed to have heard Chad say he was busy.

"I don't want —" he began, but his dad interrupted. "I'll be putting in lots of overtime the next couple of weeks. The county fair's coming, you know. We'd have to have a sitter ten or twelve hours a day."

"I can take care of myself," Chad muttered, but he'd known by then that it was settled. He was going to Milwaukee to stay with someone he didn't know. Aunt *Rosebud,* for Pete's sake! For two whole weeks he wasn't going to see anybody from Bristol except bossy, know-it-all Jeannie Nichols.

"Want some peanuts?" Jeannie put down her puzzle book and pulled a crumpled bag from her pocket.

Chad shook his head. It wasn't just his chest that hurt. His stomach felt funny, too.

"Listen, before we get to Milwaukee, I'm going to tell you about my Aunt Rosebud," Jeannie said. "She's a really great and wonderful person, but she's kind of eccentric, too."

"What's eccentric?" Chad asked grumpily.

"It means weird," Jeannie told him. "Nice-weird. You'll see when we get there. And you'd better not laugh at her, or you'll be sorry!"

Chad turned toward the window and stared out at the green fields rushing by. *Eccentric,* he thought. *Weird. Two whole weeks.*

He'd never felt less like laughing in his life.

# TWO

## *Welcome to Deadman House*

"There she is!"

Jeannie leaped from the bottom step of the bus, dragging her suitcase behind her. Before Chad could follow, she had disappeared into the crowd of passengers who filled the Milwaukee bus station.

"Hey, wait for me!"

He tried not to panic as what seemed like millions of people pushed past him. Buses snorted and roared like angry monsters, and drivers shouted over his head. Then the crowd opened up for a moment, and he caught a glimpse of Jeannie's red T-shirt. She was hugging the most astonishing-looking woman Chad had ever seen.

"Come on, pokey!" Jeannie darted back and

grabbed Chad's arm. "Aunt Rosebud, this is Chad Weldon. He's ten."

Aunt Rosebud bent down and gave Chad a hug that left him breathless. She was very tall and very wide. Her dress hung straight from her shoulders like a flowery tent, and on her head was a large pink straw hat. Dozens of pink and red roses trimmed its brim, and a bluebird peeked out from under one of them.

"I'm happy to meet you, Chad!" Aunt Rosebud's small, breathless voice didn't match the rest of her. "I'm so glad you could come with my dear Jeannie." She hugged him again, and Chad found himself looking into the bluebird's eye.

"Now come along, both of you." Aunt Rosebud scooped up their suitcases as if they weighed nothing at all. "We have to hurry. The family's waiting for dinner." She led the way out to the street, the pink hat bobbing above the crowd.

"What family?" Chad whispered to Jeannie as they climbed into the backseat of a gleaming old car. "You didn't say anything about a family." He wondered if he was going to spend two weeks with a houseful of kids like Jeannie.

She grinned. He could tell she liked being the person with all the answers. "Uncle Harold died a long time ago," she whispered back. "They only had one son, and he's grown-up and living in London. She almost never sees him."

"But she said 'family,'" Chad insisted. "Who —"

"Boarders," Jeannie said. "People who rent rooms in Aunt Rosebud's house."

Before Chad could ask another question, the car swerved wildly to the left and into the drive-through lane of a fried-chicken restaurant. It passed the microphone where customers were supposed to give their orders and screeched to a stop in front of the take-out window.

"Nice to see you, Mrs. R." The young man at the window began handing out huge bags of food as fast as Aunt Rosebud could take them. When the seat beside her was filled, she gave the man a handful of bills and stepped on the gas. The smell of hot fried chicken filled the car.

"Chicken today, hamburgers tomorrow," Aunt Rosebud sang over her shoulder. "Tacos the day after that. The world is so full of good things to eat!"

"And Chinese takeout the day after that," Jeannie said happily. "Just like the last time I was here. I love egg rolls!"

"So do I," agreed Aunt Rosebud. She took deep breaths of the chicken-scented air and looked around contentedly, as if she were a passenger, not the driver. Suddenly the car swung to the curb, and Aunt Rosebud stomped on the brake.

"Welcome to Redman House, Jeannie and Chad!" she exclaimed.

Chad blinked. "*Deadman* House?"

"Redman House, dopey." Jeannie glared at him. "That's Aunt Rosebud's name — Rosebud Redman. Don't make silly jokes."

Chad climbed out of the car and looked around him. All the houses on the block were tall and leaned together like a herd of elephants. Most of them were gray or brown, but Aunt Rosebud's was pale blue, with bright red shutters. Long red flower boxes hung from the porch railings. Above the steps a pale blue sign with red letters announced REDMAN HOUSE.

Aunt Rosebud took the suitcases out of the car trunk, and Chad and Jeannie carried the bags of food into the wide front hall of the house.

"Just drop everything in the dining room," Aunt Rosebud told them. "I'll set the table while you two go upstairs and unpack. Jeannie, you have the same room as you had the last time, at the end of the hall. Chad has the first room on the left."

Chad followed Jeannie up the stairs. The walls

were papered with a dense pattern of leaves and yellow flowers that turned the stairs into a leafy tunnel. At the top was a long hallway with many doors.

"Your room is here, and the bathroom's down there." Jeannie pointed. "Hurry up and get unpacked. I'm starving." She went down the hall, whistling.

Chad looked around him. The bedroom was at least twice as big as his room at home. There was a fireplace on one wall and two long windows on another. The walls were papered with faded blue roses as big as cabbages. A huge basket of silk flowers stood in front of the fireplace.

Chad set his suitcase on a chair and took out his clothes. Shorts, T-shirts, and underwear went into the dresser drawers. He hung his jacket in a closet that was empty except for a few boxes and some rolls of wallpaper. Then he sat down on the edge of the bed and waited for Jeannie to come back.

He felt terrible. Maybe it was because the bedroom was so different from his cozy, cluttered room at home. In spite of the silk flowers and the tall windows, it seemed gloomy and sort of damp. *I don't like it,* he thought. And another thought followed at once: *It doesn't like me, either.*

Jeannie came down the hall and peered in at him.

"Hey, you have a fireplace!" she exclaimed. "Neat!" Then she rolled her eyes. "That's a dumb place to put your toothbrush."

Chad looked where she pointed. His toothbrush was balanced on top of a bedpost. As she stared, a breeze lifted the window curtains and the brush tumbled to the floor.

Chad picked it up. "I didn't put it there," he said wonderingly. "Why would I do a goofy thing like that?"

"Who knows?" Jeannie shrugged. "Kid stuff!"

"You're only two years older than I am," Chad snapped. "You're a kid, too." But he was more puzzled than angry. He turned the toothbrush over in his hand. He knew he had put it on top of the dresser. What was going on?

As he followed Jeannie down the tunnel-staircase, his feet dragged. He didn't belong in this house; he belonged in Bristol with his family. But now he wasn't just homesick. He was scared, too.

# THREE

## *More Scared Than Ever*

The dining room was papered with lilacs and tulips. There were vases of silk flowers everywhere Chad looked.

"Here you are!" Aunt Rosebud, still wearing her pink hat, swooped into the room carrying a bowl of coleslaw and another of potato salad. She set the bowls on the table and threw her arms around Chad and Jeannie. "Are you all settled in your rooms?"

"Sure," Jeannie said.

Chad thought about his toothbrush but kept quiet.

"Mr. Bell is still out in the maple tree, I believe," Aunt Rosebud went on. "Jeannie, will you remind him that it's time for dinner, please?"

Chad followed Jeannie through the big, old-fashioned kitchen and out onto a little porch. The backyard was long and narrow, like Aunt Rosebud's house. Masses of flowers lined the fences, and in the center of the yard a maple tree spread its branches. Chad looked up in surprise at the man who sat in a crook of the tree with a guitar in his lap.

"What's he doing up there?"

"He's writing songs," Jeannie said. "He does his best work in the maple tree. Mr. Bell," she shouted, "it's time to eat."

With a quick twist of his lanky body, the man grasped the branch with both hands and dropped lightly to the ground.

"Delightful to see you again, my dear," he said. "Who is this young man?"

"Chad Weldon," Jeannie told him. "He lives across the street from me in Bristol. He's ten."

Mr. Bell shook Chad's hand. "You're a very lucky boy to have such a charming neighbor," he said. "Would you like to hear a song I wrote in her honor?"

Chad couldn't imagine anyone writing a song for Jeannie, but he nodded to be polite. Mr. Bell strummed his guitar and began to sing:

"I dream of Jeannie with the light brown hair. . . ."

Chad looked quickly at Jeannie. Her face was pink

with pleasure. Didn't she know the song had been written by someone else, a long time ago? Chad had heard Aunt Elsa sing it many times, mostly when she ran the vacuum cleaner.

"Well, what do you think?" Mr. Bell asked when the song ended.

"It's beautiful," Jeannie told him. She gave Chad a warning frown, and he realized that she *did* know the song was an old one.

"Only I don't think it fits Jeannie very well," Chad said. "I mean, it's a real nice song, but her hair is *dark* brown — sort of mud-colored."

Jeannie made a face and led the way back into the house before he could say any more. In the dining room, he saw that a platter of fried chicken had been set in the middle of the table, and two more people had joined the party.

"Sit down, my darlings!" Aunt Rosebud exclaimed. "The chicken is getting cold. Madame Keppell and Mr. Callahan, you remember my niece Jeannie. And this is her special friend Chad Weldon."

Mr. Callahan nodded without looking up from his plate. He was as pale and skinny as Madame Keppell was round. Madame Keppell smiled warmly at Jeannie and then turned to Chad with a worried expression.

"Such a sweet little boy!" she exclaimed. "But I'm afraid I see trouble all around you, my child. You must be very careful!"

"Madame Keppell tells fortunes," Aunt Rosebud explained. "But you mustn't worry, Chad. You're going to have a good time in Milwaukee — starting right now."

She pushed the platter of chicken toward him. "Eat lots, and be sure to leave room for dessert. We have a special treat tonight."

"Rosebud's desserts are famous," Mr. Bell said proudly. "Someday I'll write a song about them. She may not care about cooking, but she's the best dessert-maker in Milwaukee."

When he tasted his first bite of Aunt Rosebud's triple-fudge cake, Chad decided Mr. Bell must be right. Even Mr. Callahan, who hadn't looked up or spoken during the first part of the meal, seemed a little more cheerful as he ate his cake.

After dinner, Jeannie and Chad helped clear the table. Then they played Scrabble in the dining room, while the grown-ups, except for Mr. Callahan, sat out on the front porch.

Chad was in no hurry to go up to bed. He kept wondering which of Aunt Rosebud's boarders had played the silly trick with his toothbrush. But it had been a long day, and finally he couldn't hide his yawns.

Jeannie yawned, too. "I'm tired," she announced. "We'd better go to bed."

*Bossy as usual,* Chad thought. He followed her out to the porch to say good night, then up the leafy-tunnel stairs to the second floor.

"You're a pretty good Scrabble player," Jeannie said unexpectedly. "For a ten-year-old, I mean."

"Thanks." Chad stood at his bedroom door and watched her go down the hall. When she turned in to her room, he felt like running after her. Maybe she was bossy, but she was the only person he knew in this whole big city.

His bedroom felt chilly and unwelcoming. The blue wallpaper-roses closed in around him in the dim light of the bedside lamp. Chad looked quickly at his dresser where he'd left his toothbrush and breathed a sigh of relief. It was still there.

After a fast trip down the hall to the bathroom, he climbed into bed. He decided to leave the lamp lit, and for a while he stared into the shadowy corners of the room, unable to sleep. Finally, his eyes closed.

Later, he wasn't sure what had startled him awake. His heart thumped and he lay very still, listening to the swooshing of cars going by. Then, he felt something scratchy and damp on his ankle. He gasped and threw back the sheet. His toothbrush lay close to his foot.

How had it gotten there? Another trick, he told himself, but this one was worse. He'd been scared before, when he thought someone had sneaked into the bedroom and balanced the toothbrush on the bedpost. He was much more scared now, because he knew he hadn't moved his foot enough to touch the toothbrush.

The toothbrush had touched *him*.

# FOUR

## *Guess Where We're Going*

Chad had snatched up the toothbrush and stuffed it under the clothes in his top dresser drawer. Then he paced around the bedroom trying to decide what to do.

If he knew where the bus station was, he could be back in Bristol tomorrow evening. The thought of it made him feel better. The other half of his round-trip ticket was tucked into the neat new wallet his dad had given him just before he left. He could leave a note for Jeannie and Aunt Rosebud. That would be easier than trying to explain about the toothbrush. . . .

Explain! Chad pictured himself trying to tell his father why he'd come home. "My toothbrush kept moving around," he'd say, and his dad would say, "Very funny, son. Now, what's the real reason?" When Aunt Elsa heard, she'd be as mad as two hornets and would call him silly and ungrateful.

He'd never be able to make them understand something he didn't understand himself.

He stopped at a window and looked out. By leaning forward and looking down and a little to the right, he could see into a room in the house next door. There was a night-light on a table, and a little boy lay curled up on a bed against one wall. He had a teddy bear in his arms. He looked so cozy and safe that for a moment Chad felt a little less scared himself.

As he watched, a sad-faced young woman tiptoed into the room. She tucked the sheet around the boy and picked up a couple of toys from the floor. Then she tiptoed out again.

Chad took a shaky breath. The woman's loving look made him think of his own mom, who had died when he was six. He could barely remember her, but he bet she used to come into his room just that way and tuck the covers around him every night.

When he went back to bed at last, he fell asleep quickly. Sunshine was streaming through the windows when he woke up. He jumped out of bed and hurried to the dresser to make sure his toothbrush was where he'd hidden it.

"Chad! Wake up!" Jeannie rapped on the door. She sounded excited.

"I *am* awake," Chad mumbled. "Give me a chance to get dressed, will you?"

He waited until he heard Jeannie's footsteps clattering down the stairs, and then he took the toothbrush and went to the bathroom. In the bright sunlight the toothbrush was just a plain old toothbrush again, but Chad was still frightened. If only there were some way to make Jeannie want to go home right away! Then he wouldn't have to explain about the toothbrush to anyone.

But Jeannie was clearly happy right where she was.

"Boy, are you a sleepyhead!" she exclaimed when he entered the dining room. "Aunt Rosebud and I have been up for hours."

He and Jeannie were the only people in the dining room. Six boxes of cereal stood in a row in the center of the table, with cartons of orange juice and milk next to them.

"Aunt Rosebud's doing laundry," Jeannie reported. "Madame Keppell is telling fortunes at the Senior Center, and Mr. Callahan has gone to work.

Mr. Bell's up in the maple tree working on a song. And, guess what, you and I are going to the museum today!"

Chad filled a bowl with Krazy Krunch and added milk. "Who else is going?" he asked. Jeannie had told him at least a hundred times about all the great exhibits in the Milwaukee Museum. He guessed it would be okay to stay at Redman House one more day to see them himself.

"Why do you want to know?" Jeannie demanded suspiciously.

Chad shrugged. He didn't like to say he'd feel funny walking around the museum with Aunt Rosebud in her pink hat, or with Mr. Bell strumming his guitar.

"Well, it's just us," Jeannie told him. "I've been there three times, and Aunt Rosebud says I'll make a good guide. I know where all the best stuff is — the mummies and the buffalo and the rain forest and all that."

"Okay," Chad said. He poured some orange juice. Jeannie would be a know-it-all guide, but they would have fun. And it would be a relief to have something to think about besides a toothbrush that moved around by itself.

# FIVE

## *Someone Is Watching*

"Look, there's Aunt Rosebud." Jeannie pointed as they stepped off the bus. "She must have gone out to pick up the hamburgers and french fries for dinner tonight."

They walked down the block, watching Aunt Rosebud park and hurry into the house with a bag in each arm.

"That's the biggest, oldest, most purple car I've ever seen," Chad said. "I bet that car will be in a museum some day. An eccentric car museum."

"It's not purple, it's lilac," Jeannie told him. "Like the flower. Aunt Rosebud loves flowers."

"No kidding!" Chad grinned. His head was full of the terrific things he'd seen at the museum. It had been thrilling — even better than he'd expected. Now, with hamburgers ahead, he was glad he hadn't tried to find the bus station this morning.

"Last one home is a dinosaur!" he shouted suddenly and began to run. He had a head start, but Jeannie was very fast. They burst through the front door together, just as Madame Keppell was coming down the stairs.

"Oh, my dears, do be careful," she gasped. "Especially you, Chad. I am *so* worried about you!"

"Why?" Jeannie demanded, slowing to a walk. "He's okay."

Madame Keppell rolled her eyes. "But I see danger ahead!" she exclaimed. "And I see fear." She shook her head. "You are afraid, aren't you, Chad?"

"He's afraid there won't be enough hamburgers to go around," Aunt Rosebud called from the dining room. "Come along, you three. Mr. Bell and Mr. Callahan and I aren't going to wait much longer."

Chad's happy mood slipped away. He followed the others into the dining room with dragging feet.

"Sit here next to me, Chad," Aunt Rosebud said cheerfully. "Take two hamburgers and some potatoes, and some baked beans, too. We can pretend we're cowboys out on the prairie eating beef and beans." She winked at him. "Of course, cowboys never had Rosebud Redman's Perfect Peach Pie for dessert."

Chad knew Aunt Rosebud was trying to make him forget Madame Keppell's gloomy words. He grinned, because the idea of Aunt Rosebud as a cowboy was pretty funny. She wore a blue hat today, trimmed with butterflies that danced when she moved.

"I love the Old West," Mr. Bell said. "One of the first songs I ever wrote was about the West. 'Oh, give me a home where the buffalo roam . . .'" He helped himself to some beans. "I'll sing the rest of it later on, if you want me to."

"Of course we want you to," Aunt Rosebud said. "Chad, what did you like best at the museum?"

"The rain forest," Chad said. "When I grow up, I want to be a scientist in a rain forest. You get to sit on a platform in a treetop and study birds and butterflies and plants — "

"Don't forget the insects," Jeannie interrupted. "Those great big beetles — ugh! I like the Egyptian section best," she added, in case anyone was about to ask. "The mummies are *so* spooky! Aunt Rosebud, did you know that explorers found so many mummies in Egypt that people used them as fuel to run trains?"

Madame Keppell gasped, and Aunt Rosebud

looked as if she'd rather not have had this piece of information. "Is that so?" she said weakly. "What else did you see?"

"The Indian powwow," Chad said. "That was cool." He didn't want to talk about scary exhibits, now that he was back in a house where scary things actually happened.

Later, Aunt Rosebud came into the living room while Chad and Jeannie were watching television.

"Thank you for listening so politely while Mr. Bell sang 'Home on the Range,' " she whispered. "Each of my guests is a tiny bit unusual, but they are very dear to me. Mr. Bell makes up old songs, and Madame Keppell believes she knows what's going to happen —"

"But she doesn't really, does she?" Chad interrupted anxiously.

Aunt Rosebud patted his shoulder. "Sometimes she gets it right, and sometimes it's all wrong. I'm sure you have nothing to worry about, dear."

"What about Mr. Callahan?" Jeannie wanted to know. "He wasn't living here the last time I came."

Aunt Rosebud looked uncomfortable. "Well, Mr. Callahan has problems, too," she said slowly. "But I'm sure he's going to be fine." She looked from Jeannie to Chad, and the butterflies danced. "We all help each other. That's what families are for."

When they were alone again, Jeannie rolled her eyes. "I'd sure like to know what Mr. Callahan's problem is," she said. "I think he looks sort of — sort of *sneaky*."

Chad thought so, too, but he was more interested in Madame Keppell. It was weird being around a person who believed she could see into the future. It was especially weird when what she saw was bad.

He was still thinking about Madame Keppell's warning when they went upstairs to bed. Chad stood in the doorway of his bedroom and looked around. His toothbrush was where he'd left it on the dresser. There was nothing to be afraid of. This was a perfectly okay room except . . . except . . . *except that he felt as if someone were watching him.*

That was it! From the first moment he'd walked into the bedroom yesterday, he'd felt as if there were someone already in the room who wished he'd go away!

The closet was open a crack. Chad stared at it, and the opening seemed to grow wider. He took a step backward and held his breath.

*If you think someone's in there, there's only one way to find out, dopey.* That was what Jeannie would say. She had an answer for everything.

Chad watched the opening a moment longer. He was wrong, he decided. It hadn't gotten any wider.

Quickly, before he could change his mind, he crossed the room and threw open the door.

A mummy stood against the back wall of the closet. Its hollow eyes glared out of the shadows, and its broken teeth were bared in a terrifying grin.

# SIX

## *Mrs. Palmer's Sad Story*

"Help! SOMEBODY HELP!"

Chad hurtled out into the hall and crashed into Mr. Callahan. They fell with a thud that brought Jeannie flying out of her bedroom.

"What's going on?" she demanded. "Oh, poor Mr. Callahan!" She stepped over Chad's knees and put out a hand to help Mr. Callahan up.

"I'm okay," he said, not looking at either of them. "Just watch where you're going, boy." He scurried away and down the stairs without asking what had frightened Chad.

"You shouldn't run in the house," Jeannie said primly. "Next time you might hurt somebody."

"You'll run, too, when you see what's in my closet." Chad's voice cracked with anger and fright.

"Come on!" He pulled Jeannie into his bedroom and pointed at the half-opened closet door. "Look in there! I dare you!"

"Big deal!" Jeannie hesitated only a second. Then she marched across the room and opened the closet door wide, while Chad waited, ready to run.

"Okay, I'm looking," Jeannie said. "What am I supposed to see?"

"A MUMMY!" Chad roared. "There's a mummy right in front of you!"

"No, there isn't. I see your jacket and some clothes hangers and some boxes and rolls of old wallpaper. That's all! What's the matter with you, anyway?"

"Nothing's the matter with me," Chad said fiercely. "I saw it. It's there!"

"What's there?" Aunt Rosebud appeared, panting at the top of the stairs. Madame Keppell was right behind her.

Jeannie came out into the hall. "Chad's seeing things in his closet," she said. "He thinks he saw a mummy."

Chad ran to the closet and looked in.

"Well?" Jeannie grinned at him.

"It's gone now," Chad admitted. "But it *was* there."

"Oh, dear!" Madame Keppell moaned. "You poor child! I told you I could see trouble ahead."

Aunt Rosebud touched Chad's forehead with her fingers. "Chad's all right," she said soothingly. "Shadows can fool us sometimes, especially"— she shook her head at Madame Keppell — "especially if we've been told something bad is about to happen. You saw mummies at the museum today, didn't you, Chad?"

He nodded. He knew what she was thinking.

"Well, maybe you were remembering them, and when you opened the closet door —"

"I really saw it," Chad repeated, but now he was beginning to wonder. Was it possible that when he felt as if someone or something were watching him, his mind had tricked him into seeing a mummy?

"Will you be all right now, dear?" Aunt Rosebud asked. "Will you be able to sleep?"

"I guess," Chad mumbled. He knew he didn't want to talk about the mummy anymore.

"You don't have to be afraid," Jeannie said with a sugar-sweet smile. "I'll come right away if you start seeing things again."

When Chad opened his eyes the next morning, he felt as if he hadn't slept at all. Before going to bed, he had pushed a chair against the closet door, and every few minutes, all night long, he had gotten up to make sure it hadn't moved. Now, with sunlight streaming through the windows, and voices in the hall, he would have liked to stay in bed and sleep some more.

When he finally forced himself to go downstairs, Jeannie had finished breakfast and gone outside. Madame Keppell was eating her cereal, and Aunt Rosebud was pouring coffee.

"Jeannie is talking to Linda Palmer and little David," Aunt Rosebud told him. "They live next door. Poor girl — maybe Jeannie can cheer her up."

Chad thought of the sad-faced woman and the boy he'd seen from his bedroom window.

"What's wrong with her?" he asked.

"She's had terrible trouble," Aunt Rosebud said. "First, her husband died — that was about three years ago. Since then she's been working as a waitress, but she's not making enough money to keep David in day care all summer. It looks as if she'll have to take him to Chicago and leave him with her folks, at least until school starts."

"I warned her," Madame Keppell said suddenly. "I told her there were wicked people around her."

"What wicked people?" Chad asked uneasily.

"One of her customers at the restaurant died last March and left her a very valuable diamond bracelet," Aunt Rosebud explained. "Linda planned to sell it and use the money to keep David with her and pay off her bills. But before she could do it, someone stole the bracelet. It was a dreadful shock."

"I wasn't shocked." Madame Keppell sniffed. "I wasn't even surprised. It was just the kind of thing I was expecting."

Chad finished his cereal and drank two glasses of orange juice. Then he wandered out to the front porch, yawning and rubbing his eyes. Jeannie was sitting on the steps with a little boy.

"This is David Palmer," she said briskly. "We're going to the park — David and his mom and you and me. His mom has the day off. She's making sandwiches for us right now. Only I thought you weren't going to get up in time to go. I wanted to wake you, but Aunt Rosebud wouldn't let me. She said you probably didn't sleep very well because you were so scared."

"What are you scared of?" David Palmer asked. "I'm not scared of anything."

"Neither am I." Chad glared at Jeannie. She talked too much.

"Well, anyway, I'm glad you finally woke up," Jeannie said. "Evergreen Park is really neat. It's about ten times bigger than the park in Bristol."

Chad thought of his dad, who was probably working at Riverside Park right now. "Biggest doesn't mean it's the best," he said.

Later, though, he had to admit that Evergreen Park was pretty special. Linda Palmer had been going there since she was a little girl, and she and David knew every corner of the park. There were trails through woods, and a little stream that in one place ran right across the road when the water was high.

"Let's take off our shoes," Mrs. Palmer said. Soon they were all wading through the cold water.

When it was time for lunch, they settled at a table near the playground. Mrs. Palmer unwrapped peanut butter-and-pickle sandwiches, Chad's favorite. It turned out they were David's favorite, too.

"This is fun," Mrs. Palmer said, but even though she was smiling, there was a sad look in her eyes. "David and I do something like this whenever I have a day off. I'm going to miss him so much."

"David's going to Chicago to stay with his grandma," Jeannie explained.

"I know," Chad said. "Aunt Rosebud told me." He looked at Mrs. Palmer shyly. "She told me about the bracelet that got stolen, too."

As soon as he said it, he wished he hadn't. Mrs. Palmer's eyes filled with tears.

"I thought I'd put it in such a safe place," she said. "And it was only for a few days."

"You should have kept it in a safe deposit box," Jeannie said sternly.

"My Aunt Elsa keeps money rolled up in the toe of an old shoe," Chad said. "Where did you hide the bracelet?"

Mrs. Palmer sighed. "In David's room. It's always such a mess, I thought if a burglar broke in he'd never think of looking for something valuable in there. I put it on the high shelf over his bed, where we store old games and toys he doesn't play with anymore."

"Maybe David told someone where the bracelet was," Jeannie suggested.

"Did not!" David said firmly.

Mrs. Palmer gave the little boy a hug. "He didn't even know it was there. I just can't imagine how the thief found it."

Chad started to take another peanut butter sandwich and stopped. He stared at Mrs. Palmer. Suddenly, he was more wide-awake than he'd been all day.

"When we're through eating are we going home?" he asked. "I've got something to do."

"What's your big hurry?" Jeannie demanded.

Chad didn't answer. He wasn't going to tell her, or anyone else, what he was thinking. He just wanted to get back to Aunt Rosebud's house and check the view from his bedroom window.

# SEVEN

## *"Such a Terrible Time!"*

Chad pressed his forehead against the glass and looked down and sideways. Without a light in David Palmer's bedroom he couldn't see inside.

*I'll look tonight*, he thought. It was going to be hard to wait.

Downstairs, he found Aunt Rosebud in the kitchen frosting a cake.

"Did you have a good time at the park, dear?" she asked. Her hat today was purple, with bunches of grapes that trembled when she spoke.

"It was cool," Chad said. "Jeannie's gone to the drugstore with Mrs. Palmer, but I came home to — to look for something. And to ask you a question."

Aunt Rosebud pushed the cake to the center of the table. She handed the frosting bowl to Chad.

"There's not much left, but I bet you won't mind cleaning it up for me," she joked. She sat down and watched while Chad scraped the bowl. "What do you want to know, dear?"

"I was sort of wondering . . . who had my bedroom before me?"

Aunt Rosebud's round pink face grew serious, but she didn't seem to think it was a strange question.

"That was our poor Dr. Dempsey," she said. "It was so sad! After he retired, he invested all his money in a pickle factory and lost every last cent. He had to leave his beautiful house on the lake and rent a room here."

"He was a doctor?" Chad licked the frosting spoon.

"A dentist," Aunt Rosebud told him. "And a very good one, I'm sure. But when he came to live with us, he was an unhappy man. Pretty grouchy, to tell the truth. We all understood, of course — he'd lost so much. He couldn't even afford to keep a car. I think that was what bothered him most. And then one afternoon he went out for a walk and never came back. He was hit by a truck and killed instantly."

Chad put down the spoon. "You mean he's dead?" A shiver tickled his spine. *A dead dentist.* He thought about how *unfriendly* his bedroom felt. He thought about his toothbrush and the mummy.

"The poor man was killed last April on one of our pizza days," Aunt Rosebud said, shaking her head so that the grapes bounced wildly. "I remember because Dr. Dempsey did enjoy pizza, and that night we had a lot left over."

Chad carried the frosting bowl to the sink. He stared out into the backyard where Mr. Bell was dozing under the maple tree, his guitar across his knees.

"Do you believe in ghosts, Aunt Rosebud?" he asked softly.

"I'm not sure, dear. Do you?"

Chad nodded. "I saw one once. I wondered if you ever saw one. Or if you ever felt as if one might be hanging around."

"No, I haven't felt that way." Aunt Rosebud looked at him curiously. "Is that how you feel?"

Wild thoughts whirled through Chad's head. Dr. Dempsey was dead, but when he was alive he had wanted money. His bedroom window had looked down into David Palmer's room, where a valuable bracelet had been hidden. Maybe the two facts were connected, and maybe not. He still didn't know whether the shelf in David's room could be seen from his window.

"I sort of feel that way," Chad admitted.

He wanted to tell Aunt Rosebud what he was thinking, but later he was glad that he hadn't. When Jeannie began talking about the stolen bracelet at the dinner table that night, Aunt Rosebud didn't like it one bit.

"We know all about that business," she said, sounding surprisingly cross. "I don't think we need to discuss it again."

"Oh, dear, no!" Madame Keppell exclaimed. "It was such a terrible time. First the robbery and then Dr. Dempsey's accident. Of course, I knew bad things were about to happen, but no one listened to me. I tried to tell them —"

Mr. Callahan pushed back his chair. His face was gray, and he stood up so fast that he almost tipped over a chair. "Have to go out," he mumbled. "Sorry." He hurried from the dining room, leaving behind a plateful of tacos and beans.

"There now!" Aunt Rosebud snapped. "That's what comes of bringing up unpleasant subjects. I don't want to hear another word about Linda Palmer's bracelet."

"Okay," Jeannie said. She looked hurt. "But I don't see what everybody's so excited about."

"*I'm* not excited," Mr. Bell told her, with his usual smile. "In fact, I think I'll have another taco."

Chad felt a little sorry for Jeannie. *Maybe Aunt Rosebud knows Dr. Dempsey could have stolen the bracelet,* he thought. *Maybe she doesn't want to talk about it because he's dead.* If that was why she was upset, Chad could understand, sort of. Still, he thought if she'd told the police what she suspected, they might have talked to Dr. Dempsey and made him give the bracelet back, before it was too late.

After dinner Aunt Rosebud brought out a Monopoly board, and she and Chad and Jeannie played at the dining-room table. Chad won.

"It's because you never take chances," Jeannie said grumpily. She hated to lose.

"And you take chances all the time," Aunt Rosebud reminded her. "It's just the way you are." She smoothed back Jeannie's hair. "Right now you both look ready for bed," she said.

"I'm not," Chad said quickly. "I'm not even a little bit tired." Now that it was dark, he was no longer in a big hurry to go up to his bedroom and check the view from the window. He kept remembering the mummy in his closet. Maybe it hadn't been real, but it had *looked* real, and that was almost as bad.

"Let's play Monopoly some more," he suggested. "I'll take chances this time."

Aunt Rosebud laughed. "Tomorrow," she promised, gathering up the paper money. "But I don't know why you want to take chances, Chad. You're doing fine just the way you are."

Chad thought of that when he switched on the overhead light and closed his bedroom door behind him. He wasn't doing fine. Not at all. He stared at the closet. If he took a chance and looked inside, the mummy might be there waiting for him. If he *didn't* look, he'd lie awake watching the door, wondering. It was hard to decide which was worse.

Finally, he tiptoed across the faded carpet to the closet and clutched the doorknob with both hands, his arms stiff. Nothing happened.

He held his breath and opened the door just enough to peek inside.

The closet was empty except for the boxes and rolls of wallpaper that had been there the night before.

He closed the door and pushed the armchair across the room, so that if someone — or something — tried to come out of the closet the chair would block its way. Then he went to the window and looked down at David Palmer's window. The night-light was on, and the little boy was sleeping soundly. High above the bed, and easy to see, was the shelf Mrs. Palmer had told them about. It was jammed from one end to the other with battered game boxes and books with their covers half off.

*That should have been a safe place to hide a bracelet,* Chad thought. No one would think of looking there — unless the person had watched Mrs. Palmer put it there.

Dr. Dempsey, the dead dentist, could have seen her do it. This bedroom, where scary things happened, had been Dr. Dempsey's room. Chad undressed fast and climbed into bed. He shivered even though the breeze from the window was warm.

For a long time he tossed about, too scared to sleep. Then, just as he was finally dozing off, something moved under his pillow, close to his cheek. With a yelp of fright, he leaped up and threw the pillow on the floor.

In the faint light of the bedside lamp he saw a black shape, about the size of a mouse on the sheet. *No way!* he thought, but there it was — a huge rhinoceros beetle like the ones he'd seen at the museum yesterday. Only this beetle was bigger. Meaner looking. And it was crawling right toward him.

# EIGHT

## *"We Mustn't Be Frightened."*

Chad had raced to the bedroom door, then looked back to see if the beetle was following him. It had disappeared. He tiptoed to the bed and threw aside the covers. The beetle wasn't there. It wasn't under the other pillow, either, or under the bed itself. It had vanished, as completely as the mummy had vanished the night before.

He backed into the chair that blocked the closet door and sat down hard. His legs shook and his heart thumped like a drum.

What should he do? It was no use calling Aunt Rosebud or Jeannie. There was nothing for them to see. But he didn't dare get back into bed. Finally, he shook the blanket once more, to make sure nothing was hidden in its folds, and wrapped it around his shoulders. He would have to spend the night in the chair. That way, nothing could get out of the closet without his knowing it, and if the beetle came back — from under the mattress, maybe? — he would see it and run.

For the next couple of hours Chad stared at the rumpled sheets and pillows until his eyes burned. Once in a while he almost dozed off, but Aunt Rosebud's old house was full of creaks, and with each little sound he was wide-awake again.

He had lots of time to think. Someone, he realized, was going to a lot of trouble to scare him. The Someone had been watching him at the museum. Even though he'd enjoyed looking at the Egyptian mummies and the weird insects in the rain forest, they had made his skin crawl. Someone, or something, had known that.

When he fell asleep at last, he dreamed he was on a platform high in a jungle tree. The floor around his feet was swarming with monster beetles. When he leaned over the edge of the platform, looking for a way to escape, he saw a mummy clinging to the tree trunk and reaching upward with a bony hand.

The bedroom was full of sunlight when he woke

up. His head ached, and he was sweating under the blanket. He felt as if he'd spent the whole night trying to answer the same question: *Why should anyone want to scare me?*

He looked around the room, searching for an answer. When his eyes reached the dresser, he gasped and pulled the blanket more tightly around him. On the mirror scrawled in mint-green toothpaste, were two words:

GO HOME!

Footsteps sounded in the hall. Chad raced across the room and threw open the door, startling Aunt Rosebud.

"Chad, dear, what is it? Why are you wrapped up in a blanket on such a lovely warm morning?"

Chad pointed into his bedroom. "There," he choked. "On the mirror!"

Aunt Rosebud stepped past him, and he followed her, peeking cautiously around her hip. The mirror sparkled cleanly in the sun.

"There was writing!" Chad was close to tears. "It said, 'Go home!' Honest!"

Aunt Rosebud bent close to the mirror and smiled at the butterflies dancing on her hat. "Well, there's nothing there now," she said, as if Chad couldn't see that for himself. "But I know you think you saw something, dear," she added kindly. "Are you still worrying about a ghost?"

Chad couldn't stop looking at the mirror. "There's been other stuff besides the writing," he mumbled. "Worse stuff! That mummy in the closet. And last night there was a beetle under my pillow. It was the biggest one I ever saw!"

"Like the ones in the rain forest at the museum?"

"Bigger." He frowned. "I didn't just imagine it. I saw it!"

Aunt Rosebud patted his shoulder. "I'm sure you believe you did," she said soothingly. "And maybe we do have a ghost who's trying to scare you. If there *is* such a thing as a ghost, I guess it can make you see what it wants you to see. Madame Keppell says the spirits can do anything they wish. But if we do have a ghost, then we must just think of it as a great adventure, dear. We mustn't be frightened by a little teasing."

Teasing! Chad jerked away from Aunt Rosebud's reassuring hug. What did she mean, *we* mustn't be frightened? He was the only one being haunted.

"It's that Dr. Dempsey!" he shouted, aware that Jeannie and Mr. Bell were standing in the doorway now, listening. "He doesn't want me here. He does dumb tricks with my toothbrush and he makes me see things —"

"Oh, Chad, why would poor Dr. Dempsey want you to leave us?" Aunt Rosebud interrupted gently. "He was a *good* man under all that anger. I know it!"

Chad stared at her. It was no use. She would always believe the best about everyone. If he told her right now what he thought had happened to Mrs. Palmer's bracelet, she'd be disappointed in Chad Weldon, not poor Dr. Dempsey.

# NINE

## *Chad Plays Detective*

"You know what I think?" Jeannie asked. They were alone on the front porch after breakfast. "I think you're making up reasons to go home. You're homesick, that's what!"

Chad glared at her. He *was* homesick, and he wanted to get away from Aunt Rosebud's haunted house. But he wasn't a liar.

"It's rude to want to go home when Aunt Rosebud is trying to show us a good time," Jeannie went on, ignoring Chad's scowl. She was making red roses out of crepe paper and wire, the way Aunt Rosebud had taught her. "I guess you'd rather go back to boring old Bristol than go to the zoo for a picnic tomorrow."

"I never said that," Chad grumbled. The truth was, he'd rather go back to Bristol than anywhere else in the world, but he wasn't about to say so.

Jeannie finished another rose and added it to those already in her jelly-jar vase. "There," she said proudly. "How do they look?"

"They look like rolled-up crepe paper with wire wrapped around it," Chad said. "Who's going to the zoo besides you and me?"

"Everybody. And we're going to have sub sandwiches and Aunt Rosebud's super-fudge brownies. Unless," she added meanly, "you keep on being such a baby and Aunt Rosebud sends us home early. If that happens, I'll hate you forever."

Chad was about to say "Who cares?" when the screen door of the Palmers' house opened. Mrs. Palmer and David came out on the porch.

"We're going to the grocery store," Mrs. Palmer called. "Want to come with us?"

"I do," Jeannie shouted, the roses forgotten.

"Me, too," Chad said. He'd thought of some questions he wanted to ask about the stolen bracelet.

Luckily, Mrs. Palmer didn't mind talking about her troubles.

"Of course I remember everything about hiding

the bracelet," she said, her blue eyes filling with tears. "I picked it up at the lawyer's office in the afternoon. It was in a velvet-lined box, and it was so beautiful, I couldn't stop looking at it. I know I should have taken it to a bank right away," she went on, with a sideways glance at Jeannie, "but I've never owned anything so lovely. I wanted to keep it close to me."

"What did you do when you got home?" Chad asked. "Did you hide it right away?"

"Well, first I showed it to Rosebud," Mrs. Palmer said. "And then I put it in a kitchen drawer under some towels. When it was time to go to bed, I didn't want to leave it downstairs, so I took it up to David's room. He was sound asleep. I sat on the edge of his bed and opened the box for one more look, and then I put it on the shelf above his bed. I still can't believe a burglar would think of looking for something valuable there."

Chad had no trouble believing it. If Mrs. Palmer had stopped to show the bracelet to Aunt Rosebud, Dr. Dempsey might have seen it, too. Or he might have overheard them talking about it. Then all he had to do was look out his bedroom window at the right moment. . . .

"Did you look at the bracelet again after that?"

"Once or twice." Chad could tell that Mrs. Palmer was beginning to wonder why he was asking so many questions. "I was *not* careless," she said firmly. "No matter what anybody says."

They had reached the door of the supermarket, and David scampered ahead to get a cart.

"Are you trying to be Sherlock Holmes, or what?" Jeannie whispered. "Asking all those nosy questions!"

"I wasn't being nosy," Chad whispered back. "I'm figuring out something."

"What? You'd better tell me — ouch!" Jeannie winced as David pushed the grocery cart over her toe. "Watch where you're going, David."

But the little boy was too excited to stop. "Hey!" he shouted. "Free snacks!"

They all turned to look. A man stood behind a serving table, cutting sausage in paper-thin slices.

"It's Mr. Callahan!" Jeannie exclaimed. "Hi!"

Mr. Callahan glanced up for only a second. "Hi," he mumbled and went back to his work.

"Come on, David," Mrs. Palmer said sharply. "Don't be a pest." She grabbed the cart and pushed it and David down the aisle.

"May we have a snack?" Jeannie asked.

Mr. Callahan held out a plate without looking up.

"Would it be all right if I took one for David, too?" Jeannie asked.

Mr. Callahan nodded. His hands shook as he arranged slices of sausage on a plate of crackers.

When they caught up with the Palmers, Linda Palmer looked annoyed.

"That man is one very odd duck," she said. "He never speaks, and he never looks you in the eye."

"I think he's sneaky, but Aunt Rosebud says he's just shy," Jeannie told her. "She says all of her guests are a tiny bit unusual."

Mrs. Palmer sniffed. "Well, *he* certainly is. I've said good morning to him a dozen times, and he hardly answers. I don't trust him. He acts guilty of *something.*"

Chad looked at her thoughtfully. Mr. Callahan did act guilty. And his bedroom was just down the hall from Chad's, with only a closet between. Was it possible that more than one member of Aunt Rosebud's family could see into David Palmer's bedroom?

When Chad woke the next morning, he looked around fearfully, wondering if the ghost had returned during the night. The room was chilly and dark. Rain splattered against the windows.

*That means we're stuck in the house*, he thought gloomily. He slid out of bed and went to the window. David Palmer's bedroom light was still on, and the little boy was crouched on the floor in his pajamas, playing with a truck.

Chad dressed and went out into the hall. Mr. Callahan's door was closed, and people were talking in the dining room. He tiptoed to the top of the stairs and listened, but the only voices he heard were Aunt Rosebud's and Jeannie's.

He shifted from one foot to the other. Since Mr. Callahan spent every evening in his room, this might be the only chance to look out of his window. But what if he were still in there?

Holding his breath, he tiptoed to Mr. Callahan's door and opened it just a crack. There was no sound from inside. He peered through the opening.

Sunflower wallpaper covered the walls. There was a neatly made bed, a rocking chair, a dresser. No Mr. Callahan.

Chad slipped inside and closed the door behind him. The room was cozy and cheerful, in spite of the rain. Sunflowers were nicer than blue roses, he decided. He hurried to the windows.

Straight ahead was the gray siding of the house next door. But when he looked sideways and down — to the left instead of to the right — he could see into David's bedroom. David was still there, pushing his truck across the carpet, but his bed and the shelf couldn't be seen.

Chad sighed. He was relieved and disappointed at the same time. He stepped back from the window, then returned for one more look. This time he leaned forward till his forehead pressed against the glass. Now he could see David's dresser, cluttered with toys, on the other side of the room. Above the dresser was a tall mirror, and in the mirror — Chad's eyes widened — he could see David's bed and the shelf above it!

He hurried back to the empty hall, trying to decide what to do about his discovery. He could tell Aunt Rosebud, but then he'd have to admit he'd been in Mr. Callahan's room. It would be better, he decided, to tell Mrs. Palmer about Mr. Callahan, and about Dr. Dempsey, too. She wouldn't care how he'd found out.

He started down the stairs, just as Jeannie came running up to meet him.

"Wait'll I tell you!" she whispered. "This is really exciting!"

"What is?"

"I just answered the phone and it was for Mr.

Callahan. I told the man he'd gone to work, and the man said" — Jeannie paused — "oh, you'll never guess! The man said, 'Tell Jack his parole officer called. We have to meet at a different time next week.'"

Chad stared. "His parole officer?"

"Mr. Callahan must have been in prison, dopey. That's why he's so pale. He's probably spent half his life in jail, and now he's right here in Aunt Rosebud's house. Mrs. Palmer said he acted guilty, remember? Wait till I tell her how right she was!"

# TEN

## A Clue at the Zoo

"I know something, too," Chad said. He hadn't planned to tell his news to Jeannie, but he couldn't stop himself. "You can see into David Palmer's bedroom from Mr. Callahan's window. Dr. Dempsey could see in there, too. They both could have watched Mrs. Palmer hide that bracelet."

Jeannie sat down on a step. "The bracelet!" she exclaimed. "That's it! That's what Mr. Callahan is acting so guilty about. He stole the bracelet!"

"Or Dr. Dempsey stole it," Chad reminded her. "Either one."

"No way!" Jeannie snapped. "It had to be Mr. Callahan. He's a criminal, for Pete's sake. Besides, Dr. Dempsey is dead."

"He wasn't dead when the bracelet was stolen," Chad said. "We haven't any proof —"

"We'll find some," Jeannie said excitedly. "We'll be detectives!"

"No, we won't," Chad protested. "I'm going to tell Mrs. Palmer about the windows, that's all. She can call the police if she wants to —"

Jeannie hopped up, her eyes shining. Chad wished with all his heart he hadn't told her his news. Now he'd never be able to talk her into going back to Bristol early. *Why should she?* he thought unhappily. She wasn't the one who saw mummies and beetles in her bedroom. She didn't wake up to messages written on her mirror. Her toothbrush stayed where she put it.

"We'll search Mr. Callahan's room for clues!" Jeannie exclaimed. "Right now, while he's at work."

"No, we won't," Chad told her fiercely. "And don't you tell Aunt Rosebud I went in there. If you tell her I'll —"

He tried to think of something bad enough, but Jeannie wasn't listening.

"We'd better not get Aunt Rosebud mad at us," she said, as if she were the one who'd thought of it. "But we'll watch Mr. Callahan from now on, and as soon as he does something suspicious we can tell

Aunt Rosebud, and Mrs. Palmer, too. We'll be heroes!"

She darted back down the stairs, and Chad followed more slowly. He was hungry and he was worried. He could remember other times when Jeannie had decided they were going to be heroes. So far, it hadn't happened.

Saturday morning was warm and bright — a perfect day for the picnic at the zoo. Even Madame Keppell seemed more cheerful than usual as they climbed out of the car and looked around for an empty picnic table.

"Over there," she said, pointing at a table shaded by a big oak.

"There's an unseen guest among us," she continued as they crossed the lawn. "But I'm quite sure it can't hurt us here in this beautiful park. You must all try not to be afraid."

"We'll try," Aunt Rosebud promised. Her face shone under a hat that held all the colors of a rainbow. Chad thought she looked as if she'd never been frightened in her life.

While Aunt Rosebud and Madame Keppell set out the sub sandwiches, fresh fruit, and brownies, Jeannie, Chad, and Mr. Bell played catch.

"You're giving me an idea for a song," Mr. Bell panted after a few minutes. "I think I'll just sit down and work on it before I forget it."

"I bet it'll be 'Take Me Out to the Ball Game.'" Jeannie chuckled.

Chad threw the ball over her head and ran after her when she chased it. "Where's Mr. Callahan?" he whispered. "I thought he was going to meet us here."

"Aunt Rosebud thinks he might not come after all," Jeannie whispered back. "He *said* he had an errand to do after he finished his morning job. I can guess what it is! I wonder if Aunt Rosebud knows he has a parole officer."

If she did, Chad thought, she wouldn't care. He was glad they had decided to keep their suspicions to themselves. Detectives weren't supposed to feel guilty about their detecting, but Chad couldn't help it. Whenever he remembered how he'd sneaked into Mr. Callahan's bedroom, he felt like a thief himself.

Later, when the sandwiches were gone, and only a couple of brownies remained on a paper plate, Chad and Jeannie set out to inspect the animals.

"Stay close together, my dears," Madame Keppell called after them. "Be careful!"

Jeannie looked back with a sweet smile. "I'll take care of Chad," she promised. "Don't worry."

"You will not." Chad glowered at her.

"Yes, I will. We're going to see the elephants first. Then the lions and tigers — all the big cats. And then" — she grinned — "we'll go to the reptile house. They have snakes that could swallow a kid like you in one bite."

"Could not," Chad said, wincing. Jeannie knew he didn't like snakes.

The zoo was crowded with visitors moving excitedly from one exhibit to the next. Chad decided that if he didn't become a scientist in a rain forest someday, he'd probably be a zookeeper. He loved the bird house and the monkey island. The sliding, diving penguins made him laugh. And the lions and tigers were thrilling in their junglelike setting.

"Hey!" Chad and Jeannie both jumped backward, almost knocking each other over in their haste to get away from a sleek black panther that pressed its muzzle against the glass and snarled at them.

"Guess he likes girls with mud-colored hair," Chad said, trying to laugh. "Or maybe he doesn't like them. Maybe he wants to eat up every girl with —"

"Ha-ha, funny!" Jeannie said. She was trying to laugh, too, but her face was pale with fright. Chad guessed she'd get even with him for his joke later.

She did. By the time they reached the reptile house she was her bossy self again and insisted on stopping to study every single snake. Chad thought there must be about a million of them.

"Wow!" She pointed at a rattlesnake snoozing on a rock. "How'd you like to meet him in your back-yard?" She snickered at the look on Chad's face. "Or that one." She tapped a glass wall, and a giant boa constrictor tightened its coils.

Chad tried to think of something else. Aunt Rose-bud's hats. Aunt Elsa's chocolate-chip cookies. Mr. Bell's "new" song . . .

"That's a coral snake over there," Jeannie went on. "Aren't those colors neat? It could kill you though — just like that." She snapped her fingers.

Chad stopped trying to act cool. "I'm going back to see if Mr. Callahan showed up," he said. "You can stay here — it's okay with me."

To his surprise, Jeannie didn't argue. They left the reptile house and walked down the path toward the picnic grounds. As they crossed the road, a gleaming red motorcycle coasted past them.

"Hey!" Chad grabbed Jeannie's arm. "Look who's on that motorcycle."

It was Mr. Callahan. They watched in amazement as he slowed almost to a stop to look over the picnic grounds. When Aunt Rosebud's rainbow hat bobbed into sight, he waved and rode on.

"Where did he get it?" Chad wondered as the motorcycle picked up speed. "That's just the kind I'm going to have some day."

"You'll need lots of money," Jeannie said. "They're expensive." They looked at each other.

"Maybe he borrowed it from a friend," Chad suggested uneasily.

"Or maybe he sold something valuable," Jeannie retorted, eyes gleaming. "Something like a diamond bracelet."

# ELEVEN

## *Another Bad Night*

"What a lovely day it was!" Madame Keppell exclaimed as they sat down to their fish-and-fries dinner that evening. "Though I must admit I worried all afternoon."

"You looked as if you were sleeping," Mr. Bell commented. "Your eyes were closed."

Madame Keppell frowned. "I was certainly *not* sleeping," she said, sounding hurt. "I was using all my powers to keep harm away from the children. Chad is still in some kind of danger!"

Chad squirmed and looked over his shoulder. For a little while he'd actually managed to stop thinking about the ghost.

"I'm sure we don't need to worry about Chad,"

Aunt Rosebud said, smiling at him. "You can take care of yourself, can't you, dear?"

"I guess," Chad said, but he was becoming more mixed-up every minute. Madame Keppell kept telling him he was in danger, but Aunt Rosebud said he must think of the ghost — if there really was a ghost — as a great adventure. Grown-ups were supposed to have all the answers, but sometimes they just made things more confusing.

The evening went by too fast. Chad and Jeannie watched television for a while, and they helped Aunt Rosebud put together a jigsaw puzzle. Madame Keppell sat in a corner, looking unhappy.

"You children had better go up to bed," Aunt Rosebud said, after Chad's fifth or sixth yawn. "All that fresh air at the zoo has made you sleepy."

Chad glanced uneasily at Madame Keppell. "I'm not tired," he said. He yawned again.

"Well, I am," Jeannie said. "Come on, Chad. You can sleep in my room and I'll sleep in yours, if you're scared."

"I'M NOT SCARED!" Chad said, so loudly that Aunt Rosebud dropped a piece of the puzzle.

"Of course you are, dear," Madame Keppell murmured. "I would be, too."

Chad stood up. Going to bed in a haunted bedroom couldn't be much worse than listening to Madame Keppell worry out loud.

"Night, everybody," he called over his shoulder. He took the hall stairs two at a time and was in his bedroom with the door closed before Jeannie could catch up with him.

His toothbrush was back on the bedpost. "GO AWAY!" was printed on his mirror in big letters that faded as he stared at them. It was going to be another bad night.

Chad tried to decide what to do. So far, the ghost had played its tricks when there was no one but Chad to see them. Maybe if he left his bedroom door open, so that anyone passing by could look in . . . He undressed quickly, put on his pajamas and ran down the hall to the bathroom. When he returned, he stowed his toothbrush in the bottom drawer of the dresser and jumped into bed, leaving the hall door open wide.

A half hour later he heard footsteps on the stairs, and Aunt Rosebud and Madame Keppell came up together. Chad lay with his back to the door so they wouldn't know he was still awake. A little later he heard Mr. Bell come up, humming to himself. Mr. Callahan had gone to his room right after dinner, as usual. Silence settled over the old house, and still

Chad lay stiffly, waiting, almost afraid to take a deep breath.

Maybe, he thought, the open door had been a good idea. Then he heard a small scratching sound. It came from the closet.

*It's a mouse,* he told himself, his heart pounding. He sat up in bed, clutching the sheet around him, and stared at the closet door. *Just a mouse . . .*

The door flew open. A great black shape — a panther! — sprang into the circle of light from the bedside lamp. For a moment it glared at Chad, all fangs and gleaming red eyes. Then it crouched and leaped through the window.

Chad jumped out of bed. He slammed the window and the closet door and dragged the chair across the room to block the closet. Then he scrambled back into bed and waited for whatever might happen next.

"What's wrong with you, dopey?" Jeannie peered in at him from the hallway. "Why are you making so much noise?"

"There was a —" He stopped. A panther in his bedroom sounded silly, even to him. Jeannie would say he was making up another story so Aunt Rosebud would send him home.

He gulped. "Nothing's wrong," he said. "Go to bed."

She rolled her eyes at him and went back down the hall to her room.

Chad took deep breaths and tried to calm down. The panther hadn't been real. He knew that. But someone — the ghost — had seen him jump when the panther at the zoo snarled at him. And if the ghost had seen that, then he must have been with them all day — the unseen guest Madame Keppell kept talking about. . . . Chad shuddered at where his thoughts were taking him.

There was rustling under the bed. *That's not a mouse,* he thought. He was pretty sure he knew what it was. The rustling grew louder, and the huge flat head of a snake appeared at the foot of the bed. Chad pulled his knees up to his chin and watched in horror as a long rippling body slid into view. Coil upon coil, it gathered itself on the foot of the bed. Its long tongue licked toward Chad's knees.

*That's not real either!* Chad hugged himself to keep from screaming. But it looked real. It looked as real as any one of the million or more snakes Jeannie had made him look at that afternoon.

Suddenly he couldn't watch that flicking tongue for another second. He leaped out of bed and dashed into the hall. His bare feet flew over the flowered carpet and down the stairs to the shadowy rooms below. Not daring to look back, he raced through the dining room and out into the kitchen. His trembling fingers found the switch and flooded the big room with light.

The telephone was on the counter. He snatched it up and dialed, listening to the far-off ring in his very own house in Bristol.

"Hello?" His dad sounded sleepy and a little bit cross. Chad glanced at the clock on the kitchen wall. It was just past midnight.

"Hi," he whispered. "It's me."

"Chad?" Now his dad seemed a little more awake. "Do you know what time it is? What's wrong?"

Chad thought about the snake on his bed upstairs. He thought about the panther that had leaped through his screened, second-story window. It was no use trying to tell his father about *them.*

"I want to come home," he whispered hoarsely. "I don't like it here. I want to come home tomorrow."

"Chad, you can't." Now his dad was fully awake. "Aunt Elsa won't be back for another week, and I'm working ten-hour shifts. We'd have to hire a sitter, and there's no money for it. You hang in there."

Chad peeked around the edge of the door to make sure the snake hadn't slithered down the stairs after him.

"You still there, buddy?"

"Yeah."

"Well, listen," his dad said earnestly. "Jeannie's mom tells me Aunt Rosebud is a great old girl. Is that right?"

"Yeah." Chad was clutching the phone so hard that his fingers ached. "She's okay."

"So you talk to her when something goes wrong, buddy. And don't let little stuff bother you. Okay?"

*Little stuff!* Chad thought. But he knew it was no use arguing. He was stuck right where he was until Aunt Elsa came home.

# TWELVE

## *A Very Weird Accident*

Chad was asleep at the kitchen table when Aunt Rosebud came downstairs the next morning.

"What in the world are you doing here, dear?"

He blinked up at her sleepily. In the morning sunshine last night was like a bad dream.

"I couldn't fall asleep," he said.

"Were you hungry?" she asked, looking concerned. "You should have had a brownie and a glass of milk before you went to bed."

"It wasn't that." Chad thought about what his dad had said on the phone. Maybe Aunt Rosebud would be able to help him, after all.

"I was just wondering," he said, "is there someplace else where I could sleep? I mean, do you have a room you aren't using?"

"Not a one," Aunt Rosebud said cheerfully. "Really, dear, you have one of the nicest bedrooms in the house. But I know what we can do," she went. "If you aren't comfy in there, Jeannie offered to exchange with you. We'll talk to her at breakfast."

"NO!" Chad jumped up in alarm. "That's okay. It doesn't matter." He was suddenly aware that his feet were bare and he was wearing pajamas. He had to get upstairs fast, before Jeannie appeared and found out he'd slept in the kitchen.

"Don't say anything to her, okay?"

Aunt Rosebud nodded. "If that's what you want, dear," she said, "but I know she'd be glad to help."

Chad hurried upstairs. The hall was empty, and all the bedroom doors were closed. Cautiously, he opened his own door and peeked inside. The snake was gone. His toothbrush was on the chair in front of the closet.

During breakfast Chad felt Aunt Rosebud watching him. She had worry-wrinkles in her forehead.

"How would you two like to go swimming today?" she suggested, when they'd finished their cereal. "I can drop you off at a city pool not far from here, and you can walk home when you're ready."

"Cool!" Jeannie exclaimed. "I've got a new swimsuit."

"Chad?" Aunt Rosebud smiled at him. "You brought swimming trunks, didn't you?"

"Sure," Chad said. "Old ones."

Aunt Rosebud, Madame Keppell, and Mr. Bell all laughed, as if he'd said something funny. Even Mr. Callahan smiled, a little.

"Well, then, it's settled," Aunt Rosebud said. "What a perfect way to spend a summer day!"

*And a good way to get out of the house for a while,* Chad thought. He would have said yes to anything Aunt Rosebud suggested.

The pool was the biggest Chad had ever seen. The blue water sparkled invitingly — what they could see of it.

"There's too many people!" Jeannie moaned, peering through the high fence. "There's no room to swim."

"Sure there is," Chad said quickly, before she decided she wanted to go home. "It just looks crowded from out here."

"It *is* crowded."

Chad grabbed her hand and tugged. "I'm going in," he said. "Don't you want to wear your new suit?"

To Chad's relief, she let herself be pulled toward the gate.

The pool was even more crowded than it had seemed from outside the fence, but the water was cool and everyone was good-natured. For a while Chad and Jeannie raced each other from one side of the shallow end to the other, ducking under arms and around legs. Then a boy asked Chad if they wanted to play water ball. That was fun, too. Between games they stretched out on the concrete and baked in the sun.

"This has been the best day so far," Jeannie commented, late in the afternoon.

Chad agreed. He felt safe in the crowd of laughing, jostling swimmers.

"But we'd better go home now," Jeannie went on. "I'm starving. I haven't had anything but an ice cream bar since breakfast." And this time she couldn't be talked out of leaving.

With every step of the walk home, Chad grew more unhappy. When they turned at last into the street before Aunt Rosebud's, he was hot, hungry, and cross.

"Look!" Jeannie said unexpectedly. "There's Mr. Callahan's motorcycle. In front of that computer store. Let's see if he's inside."

"What do we care?" Chad grumbled.

"We're checking up on him, dopey," Jeannie said

impatiently. "We have to find out if he's spending more money."

When Chad didn't move, she ran up to the store window and peered inside. "He *is* buying something," she reported excitedly. "A clerk is showing him a computer this very minute."

"Maybe he's looking at them because he wishes he could have one," Chad said. He remembered how many times he'd hung around the bicycle store at the mall, before he got a new bike of his own.

"We have to find out," Jeannie said. "Oh, *no!* He's coming. Run!" She dashed around the side of the store and flattened herself against the brick wall.

Chad followed, unwillingly. "What difference does it make if he sees us?" he demanded. "He doesn't know we're checking up on him."

Jeannie didn't answer. A moment later they heard the motorcycle's growl, and Mr. Callahan drove off down the street.

"That was close," Jeannie said. "Let's go in and ask the clerk if he bought anything."

"No!" Chad started toward the corner without waiting to see if she followed. If Mr. Callahan was the thief who stole Mrs. Palmer's bracelet, he deserved to be caught, but Chad didn't feel like spying on him anymore. He just wanted to get through the next few days and go home. When Jeannie caught up and called him a quitter, he pretended he didn't hear.

For dinner that evening they had a bucket of fried chicken, mashed potatoes, a whole platter of raw vegetables, and for dessert, Aunt Rosebud's strawberry cheesecake. Some boxes were delivered for Mr. Callahan, just as they were finishing the cheesecake.

"It's a computer and a printer and a whole bunch of other stuff," Jeannie whispered to Chad. She had raced to answer the doorbell and had a look at the boxes before Mr. Callahan carried them upstairs. "I told you so!"

Madame Keppell cleared her throat. "There's something I would like to do this evening," she announced. "I think we should have a séance and try to contact the spirits. We must help Chad. There is danger all around him."

They all looked at Chad. "I don't see anything," Jeannie said.

"Well, it's there," Madame Keppell insisted. "And we ought to find out what this threatening spirit wants."

Chad knew what it wanted. It wanted him to go home.

"No séance," Aunt Rosebud said firmly. "I believe it's all this talk about spirits and danger that is upsetting Chad, dear Madame Keppell. You know I have great respect for your powers, but — no séance." Her lavender hat, with clusters of pansies tucked around the brim, bobbed furiously.

"Look out!" Mr. Bell shouted. They jumped as a pottery bowl full of silk flowers flew off the top of the china cabinet, just missing the lavender hat. The bowl crashed in the middle of the dinner table, scattering flowers in every direction.

"There!" Madame Keppell exclaimed. "Now will you believe me? A very wicked spirit, indeed!"

"Nonsense!" Aunt Rosebud stared at the wreckage. "The bowl was too near the edge of the cabinet, that's all. There's no need to get excited."

Mr. Bell stood up, looking scared. "You'll have to excuse me," he said and snatched up his guitar from behind his chair. "I have work to do." He hurried to the kitchen and out the backdoor, moving faster than usual.

"Well, now," Aunt Rosebud said cheerfully. "No real harm done. Let's clean up the table, and then we'll get out some games and have a pleasant evening together." She collected the pieces of the bowl and the flowers. Madame Keppell stacked the dinner plates, muttering to herself as she carried them to the kitchen.

Chad was still too startled to move. He looked at Jeannie, who was staring at the top of the china cabinet.

"That bowl wasn't near the edge," she said after a moment. "And it didn't fall down, it fell sideways. I never saw anything fall sideways before. It was very weird."

*More than weird,* Chad thought. Maybe if his dad knew bowls of flowers were flying around Aunt Rosebud's house, he would call Aunt Elsa and tell her to come home from Duluth right now.

# THIRTEEN

# "This Whole House Is Going Crazy!"

"I don't feel like playing games," Madame Keppell pouted. "I'm going up to my room and read."

"Oh, dear." Aunt Rosebud sighed. "I've hurt her feelings, and I didn't mean to do that. It's just that all that talk about evil spirits and danger — well, I wish that once in a while she had some *good* news."

"Chad and I have news about Mr. Callahan," Jeannie said. She gulped. "Not good news, I guess."

"Then I don't want to hear it," Aunt Rosebud said at once. "I'm going up to Madame Keppell to tell her how sorry I am. I can't bear for her to be unhappy."

"Now what?" Jeannie demanded, when they were alone. She looked ready to burst. "Between Mr.

Callahan and your ghost this whole house is going crazy!"

"It's not my ghost," Chad snapped. He watched moodily as Jeannie went to a window and looked out. "Mrs. Palmer's over there on her porch watching David ride his tricycle," she reported. "Let's tell *her* what we found out."

Surprisingly, Mrs. Palmer wasn't interested in hearing about Mr. Callahan, either.

"Next week I'm going to have to take David out of day care and leave him with my folks in Chicago," she said unhappily. "That's all I can think about. Maybe Mr. Callahan stole my bracelet and sold it, or maybe it was someone else. Either way, David won't be here with me. We won't be a family anymore. Catching the thief won't change that."

Her voice grew louder; she sounded as if she were going to cry. Chad glanced over his shoulder, hoping Aunt Rosebud was still upstairs with Madame Keppell. She'd be more upset than ever if she thought he and Jeannie had made Mrs. Palmer cry. To his dismay, Mr. Callahan was standing just inside the screen door of Redman House. He stepped back quickly when he saw Chad looking at him.

"What?" Jeannie demanded. "What's wrong?"

"It was Mr. Callahan. I think he heard what we were saying."

Jeannie looked worried for a moment. Then she shrugged. "It doesn't matter. Now he knows he isn't fooling everybody."

"But he looked really sad," Chad said uncomfortably.

"He's not as sad as Mrs. Palmer is," Jeannie retorted. "Are you sure you don't want to call the police?" she coaxed.

"You don't have a speck of real proof," Mrs. Palmer said flatly. "And if I don't have proof, I'm not going to accuse anyone. Rosebud would never forgive me."

That silenced Jeannie. Chad was relieved. He doubted that Aunt Rosebud could stay angry with anyone, even if she tried, but he didn't want to find out.

When he went up to his room that night, Chad didn't expect to sleep. First he turned on the lamp next to his bed. Then he closed the bedroom door and pushed the chair in front of the closet. After that, he piled up the bed pillows and settled back against them with all his clothes on. If he had to escape again tonight, he wasn't going to be wearing pajamas.

The room was warmer than usual, and clammy. Chad opened the book he'd brought from home and tried to read, but it was hard to keep his mind on the story. At the end of every sentence he checked the room, studying the closet door, the dresser, even the blue-rose wallpaper. Finally he gave up and closed the book.

He looked at his watch. Only ten minutes had passed. How was he going to get through this long night? Count the roses, maybe?

A thin mist drifted through the open windows and settled to the floor, partly covering the wallpaper under the sill. Chad leaned forward. The mist was thickest in one spot, almost covering a rose that seemed a darker blue than the flowers around it. He'd never noticed that before, but he'd never looked at the roses carefully either. As he strained for a better look, the mist thickened into a white fog that rolled swiftly across the floor.

A knock on the door make Chad jump.

"It's me," Jeannie whispered. "I have to talk to you."

Without waiting for an answer, she let herself in. The door swung shut behind her.

"Are you okay?" she demanded. "I was thinking about that bowl falling and I wondered — not that I believe your silly ghost stuff, but still —" She eyed Chad, who sat frozen in the middle of the big bed. Then she saw the fog streaming through the windows.

"What's that?" Her voice quavered.

"I don't know," Chad gasped. "I was looking at one of those yucky blue flowers and all of a sudden —"

"Which flower?" Jeannie wanted to know. "There's a million of them, and they're all yucky."

Chad couldn't tell her. By now, the fog had completely hidden the wallpaper beneath the window.

# FOURTEEN

## *The Hiding Place*

Chad ran to the bedroom door. He wrenched the knob as hard as he could, but it didn't turn.

"Chad!" Jeannie shrieked behind him. "There's a bat in here!"

Chad turned just as something prickly scraped his ear. "It's not a bat, it's my toothbrush!" he yelled. "Watch out!"

The toothbrush shot through the billows of fog like a small rocket, then zoomed upward and smacked Jeannie in the face.

"Ouch!" She clapped a hand over one eye and stumbled backward against the chair Chad had wedged in front of the closet door. The chair tumbled over, and the closet door flew open. A giant snake slithered out, its head poking through the fog, its long tongue flicking.

"EEEE!" Jeannie's scream was almost as frightening as the snake.

"It isn't real!" Chad shouted. He shook the doorknob again, and Jeannie leaped onto the bed. Her screams grew louder as the snake slithered across the sheets and disappeared into the fog on the other side.

"Jeannie dear! Chad! What's going on in there?" Aunt Rosebud, out in the hall, sounded frantic. Chad realized he wasn't the only person trying to open the door. The knob moved in his hand as Aunt Rosebud struggled to turn it.

"I'm going to jump out the window!" Jeannie shrieked. She looked scared enough to do it.

"Don't be dumb!" Chad shouted. "That's what he wants. He wants to scare us so much we'll go away and never come back."

"Who?" Jeannie wailed. "The snake?"

Chad ducked as the toothbrush banged into his forehead. "It's something to do with that blue flower," he shouted. "The dark one. That's what made him start —" He ran across the bedroom to the window, trying not to think about what might be hiding in the fog that billowed around his knees.

There was a crash as the mirror above the dresser slipped from its hooks and fell on the floor. The shade of the bedside lamp flew into the air and circled the room like a miniature spaceship. Dresser drawers opened and closed and opened again. Chad's T-shirts danced through the air.

Out in the hall, other voices had joined Aunt Rosebud's.

"I knew it!" Madame Keppell sobbed. "Danger, danger, danger!"

"Oh, dear, what can the matter be?" Mr. Bell cried.

"Chad," Aunt Rosebud called. "Jeannie, are you all right?"

Chad knelt at the windows and ran his fingers over the wallpaper beneath the sills. The fog was too thick for him to see what he was doing, but he could feel a bumpy place in the wall.

"Chad, the bed pillows are moving!" Jeannie shrieked. "Something's under them!"

"Don't look!" Chad shouted, but he was too late. Jeannie hurtled off the bed and landed on the floor at his side. "Beetles!" she squealed. "Humongous beetles!"

Chad grabbed her hand. "Feel the wallpaper right here," he urged. "One of the roses is pasted on top of the rest. Like a patch. We have to get it off."

"No, we don't!" Jeannie yelled. "We just have to get out of here." But she let Chad move her hand over the wall.

"Something's under there," Chad panted. "Come on, help me get the paper off."

"Don't be frightened!" Aunt Rosebud shouted, sounding terrified herself. "Mr. Callahan knows all about locks, and he's going to get you out. Be brave!"

Chad pushed away the tube of toothpaste on his shoulder and swatted the comb that was scratching the back of his neck. "Hurry up!" he told Jeannie. "Don't just sit there."

"But why are we doing this?" Jeannie demanded. "There's a snake in this room. There are beetles as big as — as *horses* running around. Why are we doing this?"

"Because," Chad said and kept scratching at the wallpaper.

"Oh, no!" Jeannie moaned. "The flowers!"

Chad glanced over his shoulder in time to see the bouquet of silk flowers rising in front of the fireplace. The flowers hovered in the air and then showered down over them like red, green, and yellow fireworks.

"GO AWAY!" Jeannie jumped to her feet and swung her arms like a windmill, scattering flowers in every direction. "GO AWAY, WHOEVER YOU ARE!"

There was a crash as the bedroom door flew open and hit the wall. Mr. Callahan burst into the room with Aunt Rosebud, Madame Keppell, and Mr. Bell right behind him. They stared in astonishment as the last of the silk flowers dropped from the ceiling into the thinning fog.

"Oh, Aunt Rosebud!" Jeannie flung herself into her aunt's arms. "It was awful!"

"Look what's here," Chad said hoarsely. He was still crouched next to the wall.

For the first time he could see what the fog had hidden. A piece of cardboard was fitted snugly into the wall where the paper was torn away. He tried to get it out with his fingernails.

"I'll do it," Mr. Callahan offered. He brushed aside a red silk tulip and knelt beside Chad. With the screwdriver he'd used to open the door, he loosened the cardboard. Behind it was a narrow opening.

"Go ahead, boy," Mr. Callahan said. "See what's in there. You found it."

Chad's fingers shook as he reached into the hole and brought out a cloth-covered box. He flicked open the little gold clasp. A narrow diamond bracelet glittered up at them from a bed of blue velvet.

"Dempsey," Mr. Callahan said softly. "I always wondered if he was the one."

"Oh, no!" Aunt Rosebud exclaimed. "Oh, no, I can't believe it. Not one of our family!"

Jeannie knelt to touch the diamonds with a wondering finger. Then she jumped up and looked around nervously. "There was a snake in here, Aunt Rosebud. Honest! And great big beetles. *Horrible* big beetles!"

Madame Keppell nodded. "I told you so," she said. "A wicked spirit at work!"

"I told you, too," Chad said. But saying it didn't feel as good as it was supposed to. Aunt Rosebud looked so sad.

For a few moments they all stared at the bracelet and at each other. Then Aunt Rosebud cleared her throat.

"We must clean up this room," she said. "Flowers and clothes all over the place! And your toothbrush up on the bedpost, Chad!"

"Do you need me?" Mr. Bell asked. "I have just had the most marvelous idea for a song. Those diamonds are like stars shining in a blue velvet sky, don't you think? So beautiful! I want to write about them."

"You go right ahead, my dear," Aunt Rosebud said. "Before you forget."

"Thank you," Mr. Bell said gravely. "I think this may be one of my best."

He wandered out of the room, singing softly to himself: "Twinkle, twinkle, little star. . . ."

Suddenly they all began to laugh, even Aunt Rosebud, who had been close to tears. Even Mr. Callahan.

# FIFTEEN

## *Part of the Family*

"Chad, you are the smartest, bravest boy I've ever known," Linda Palmer said solemnly. She sat at Aunt Rosebud's dining room table with David asleep on her lap. The bracelet, in its velvet-lined box, lay in the center of the table. Everyone was there except Mr. Bell, who was strumming his guitar upstairs, and Mr. Callahan, who had patted Chad on the head and gone back to bed.

Chad's face felt hot. "Jeannie helped," he mumbled. "But we were both real scared," he added honestly.

Jeannie looked annoyed. "I wasn't scared," she said. "Not one bit. And what I'd like to know is why Dr. Dempsey cared whether Chad might find the bracelet in his bedroom. I mean, what difference did it make now that he's dead?"

"Oh, it made a difference," Madame Keppell said at once. "Dr. Dempsey was not a nice man, but even so, he didn't want us to know the wicked thing he'd done. Especially Rosebud. He was ashamed of himself. Ghosts can be ashamed of themselves, just like anyone else," she added firmly. "I know."

Aunt Rosebud sighed and stood up. "I think we should put the bracelet in my bedroom safe overnight, Linda. Is that all right with you? You can start looking for a buyer in the morning."

Mrs. Palmer nodded happily.

"And I think Chad is the person who should put the bracelet in the safe," Aunt Rosebud went on. "We'll do it together. You carry the box, dear. You'll feel better when you see it locked away."

Chad picked up the jewelry box, closed it carefully, and followed Aunt Rosebud upstairs. At the door of his bedroom they stopped and looked in. The flowers were in their vase; the T-shirts had been folded and put away. Chad's toothbrush, toothpaste, and comb were back on the dresser. Only the hole in the wall beneath the window was left to remind them of what had happened less than an hour ago.

"It's a good thing I have extra rolls of this lovely wallpaper in the closet," Aunt Rosebud said. "I'll cover that hole tomorrow."

Chad didn't say anything.

"If you'd like, I'll sleep in here tonight, and you can have my bed," Aunt Rosebud offered.

"That's okay," Chad said. "I'm not scared now."

"But something's still worrying you. I can tell."

Chad checked to be sure Mr. Callahan's door was tightly closed. "Jeannie and I thought it was Mr. Callahan who stole the bracelet," he whispered. "We *sort of* thought so, I mean. I'm really sorry."

"That's exactly why I didn't want any talk in this house about the robbery." Aunt Rosebud led the way into her bedroom and closed the door. She opened the wall safe hidden behind a flower painting.

"Mr. Callahan was in prison for three years," she went on, "but since then he's been working at two or three jobs to earn enough for the things he wants. He was very upset when this bracelet was stolen, because he was sure he'd be suspected. The police did question him but, of course, they didn't have any proof that he did it. And you can be sure I told them what a hardworking man he is!" She sounded fierce. "He and Dr. Dempsey were both members of my family, but Dr. Dempsey is the only one who ever disappointed me."

As she said that, the bedroom door flew open and the jewelry box sailed out of Chad's hands. It hovered for a moment in front of him, and then it glided smoothly into the safe, like a toy airplane making a landing.

"Well!" Aunt Rosebud gasped. "Well, there you are! Madame Keppell was right this time. That poor unhappy man *is* sorry for what he did, and we must forgive him." The butterflies on her hat danced as she dabbed at her eyes and closed the door of the safe.

Chad had a lump in his throat. He guessed Aunt Rosebud was the best person he knew, next to his dad and Aunt Elsa.

"You have a nice family," he said softly.

"I make do." Aunt Rosebud put her arm around him. "And you're part of my family, Chad Weldon, for as long as you want to be. I know you miss your dad and aunt, but they'll be waiting when you get home. And right now you have us — and an air show tomorrow, and a boat ride around the harbor the next day. After that — well, do you think you can bear to stay at Redman House a little bit longer?"

"Sure," Chad said. He decided Aunt Rosebud was teasing him just a little, so he teased her right back. "I can stay," he said, "but I'm not sure about Jeannie. She might start getting homesick. You know how she is."

"Oh, I do," Aunt Rosebud assured him. And they giggled all the way down the stairs.